A Doctor SECOND CHANCE for the RANCHER

dobi daniels

Luxhaven
Publishing

ISBN paperback, 978-1-958987-17-9

Interior Design by Luxhaven Publishing

Cover Design by The Book Brander Boutique

Editing by JD Book Services

Proofreading by Lisa Lee Proofreading

To JC, Grandma D, and DC, whom I love more than life itself.

Standalone

Her Billionaire Nemesis (short story)

SEE ALL OF DOBI DANIELS BOOKS

at https://dobidaniels.com

AUTHOR'S NOTE

Thank you for choosing A DOCTOR SECOND CHANCE FOR THE RANCHER. I enjoyed writing the story of Maggie Fields and Peter Taylor, two very fun characters!

It's so easy to believe you may never get a second chance at love as life passes you by. I pray A DOCTOR SECOND CHANCE FOR THE RANCHER gives you the hope to believe that love is still possible no matter what age you are in life.

Please continue this journey with me in A DOCTOR BLIND DATE FOR THE COWBOY, which is the story about Dex, Max's brother. You can grab your copy at https://dobidaniels.com.

Thank you again for your support!

Dobi Daniels

A Doctor

SECOND CHANCE

for the RANCHER

r. Peter Taylor blinked twice as if in a trance as four hooves flew toward him. He ducked at the last minute, but he still ended up flat on the cobblestone driveway in front of the ranch's main house, the four black hooves narrowly missing his head. It had to be a dream, right?

"Oh, my goodness! Are you alright?" asked a soft but confident voice with a hint of a Bostonian accent. "Ornie, shoo."

It was definitely not a dream as Peter watched his assailant—a black goat with frosted ears—gobble up what looked like a cookie from the ground, shake its head, and then prance away like nothing had happened.

"Are you okay?" the person asked again.

Peter swung his eyes toward the voice that had spoken.

His eyes widened, and his response froze in his throat.

In that moment, his world as he'd known it tilted. Everything around him faded away, except for the one woman standing in front of him.

Maggie Fields. The last person he'd imagined finding here. She'd exited his life over thirty-two years ago, shattering his heart into shards. Now, here she was, still as stunning as ever with short, silvery hair that framed her graceful features—any imperfections that had come with age making her even more perfect—gazing down at him with those soft brown eyes that had always had a way of piercing deep into his soul.

Then he heard the sharp inhale, and his heart pounded like a hammer against his rib cage, as if it could exit any minute. She'd recognized him!

And that was how Peter met the one woman he'd never thought he'd ever see again in the most unimaginable way ever—his sunglasses askew, and his butt squashing a pile of horse dung.

"Peter?" she asked, her voice quivering. "What are you doing here?"

Peter didn't know whether to laugh or cringe in embarrassment.

That, precisely that, was the question of the century.

CHAPTER 2

FIVE HOURS EARLIER

"*D*ad, what's going on?"

"What do you mean?" Peter asked his son, Ian, over the speakerphone as he stuffed papers from his desk into his custom brown satchel.

"It's not like you to not tell us where you're going."

"I'm just going to get some fresh air, Son. It's not a big deal."

"It is when you haven't been returning my calls," Ian countered.

But Peter had. Just not in the way Ian had expected. "I left you a message."

"It's not the same, Dad, and you know it. It's like you're avoiding me."

Peter paused. He hadn't been evading him. He'd

just needed some time to think through some stuff, and Ian liked to check in often. "Why would I do that? I've just been busy."

"Dad, I'm just worried about you," Ian responded in a concerned tone.

Sighing, Peter dropped the papers in his hands and picked up the phone. Ian was a tad protective, and Peter understood why—Ian had taken the loss of his mother sixteen years ago much harder than his sister. But Peter had no plans to die soon, unless it was the Lord's will.

"Son, I'm fine," he replied softly.

"Stella said you haven't been eating."

Peter rubbed the back of his neck and perched on the edge of his desk. Trust Stella, his house-keeper, to be on his case. Sure, he hadn't been eating much, but he'd been busy. When he was in the zone, Peter had a tendency to get lost in his research and forget everything else, and that included the need for food. "I've had my hands full lately. I'll eat more now."

"You still won't tell me where you're going?"

"What if I checked in with you at the end of the day? Would that work?"

"Okay," Ian acquiesced.

"Thanks, Son. I'll talk to you later. Say hello to

Bella for me." Bella, short for Isabella, was Ian's two-year-old daughter.

"I will. Alright, Dad." Then the call ended.

Peter dropped the phone on his desk and rubbed his forehead. He had his reasons for not wanting to tell anyone where he was going. It would lead to questions, ones he couldn't answer now.

He ran his hand through his short salt-and-pepper hair. Lately, Peter's mind had been all over the place. It was a miracle he'd been able to wrap up his latest research paper and send it off for publication. Working as a general surgeon at one of New York's leading hospitals, Peter had risen through the ranks until he'd become one of the most sought-after surgeons in the state. He'd even bagged an excellence award a few days ago, and there was talk that they'd vote him onto the hospital board soon.

But all these wonderful pieces of news hadn't brought as much joy to him as he'd have expected. Instead, Peter had grown weary and restless and couldn't imagine living the same way for the next couple of years. Maybe he was lonely and yearned for a companion to share the rest of his life with. He'd had a wonderful marriage with his wife, but Peter had lost her after fourteen years of marriage and chosen to remain single ever since. Raising his children had been a priority for him, and he'd known how hard it was to find that kind of love again. The kind he'd experienced the first time…

Peter shook his head. No, he couldn't think about her—his first love, who he'd given his whole heart to, only for her to rip it into shreds in return. It had taken the patience and love of his beloved wife, whom he'd met two years later, for his heart to heal. He'd been luckier than most—two loves in a lifetime was more than enough. There was no point in being greedy for more.

Still, he couldn't imagine continuing his life the way it was going. He'd thought about retiring early, but dropping everything in his life was a decision Peter couldn't take lightly, given how long he'd worked hard to get to where he was. He needed to talk to someone he trusted, and a long chat with his mentor, Dr. Horatio Pearson, seemed to be what he needed.

Dr. Pearson had retired a few years ago and moved to be closer to his children and grandchildren, which was why Peter had taken today and tomorrow off and was here in his home office grabbing the few papers he thought he might need before heading out to his mentor's place a six-hour drive away.

He glanced at his Rolex. It was time to leave if he

wanted to get there on time. Peter stuffed the remaining papers in his satchel, hung it over his shoulder, and left his office.

And prayed the journey would give him the answers and peace he desperately needed.

"Ugh! Not now!" Peter turned the ignition one more time, but the car didn't even bother giving him the vroom sound he expected. It was like it had decided to collapse, and nothing could make it move. It was a good thing Peter had managed to pull it off to the side of the road before it gave up.

He dropped his head on the steering wheel. Maybe it was his fault for believing the car would survive the six-hour drive. His kids had been on his case forever to change his car, but his white BMW was his old companion—it was the first car he'd bought when he'd gotten married thirty years ago, and he'd been reluctant to part with it especially after his wife passed on. Was he expected to discard an old friend just because it was out of fashion? The car had served him well over the years, and Peter had done his part to stay on top of its maintenance checks and keep it purring. It had never disappointed him.

Until today.

Now here he was, four hours into his journey, and the car had decided it'd had enough. No warning signs whatsoever. Still, Peter couldn't abandon it here on the roadside—they'd come too far together for him to even think about it.

Sighing, he extracted his phone from the GPS dashboard mount and dialed roadside assistance. A double beep and then silence greeted him in return. He checked the upper left corner of the phone for the network signal strength, but only a 'No Service' alert glared back at him. He dialed again, hoping to get connected to roadside assistance through a nearby network like he'd heard was possible, but the second and then third attempt produced the same result.

Peter collapsed back on the headrest. Just his luck —when he'd thought things couldn't get any worse. He would have considered waiting for another passing vehicle and flagging it down for help, but he hadn't seen a single one since he'd gotten on the road with the sign that said "Welcome to Dexin Valley" ten minutes ago, which was surprising considering how well-maintained the road was.

He'd only taken this road because GPS had high-lighted it as a much faster route to his destination. Now, it seemed it might have been better getting stuck in the middle of a busier highway than a back road with flowering meadows and majestic mountains in the background—he would have gotten help by now.

Peter rubbed the back of his neck. There was no point wasting time here. He had to keep moving if he didn't want the trip to be a waste. It was only by some miracle he'd gotten some free time, and he needed to make the most of it.

He put on his sunglasses, hopped out of the car, and looked around. There were acres of fenced-in land on either side of the road, but he could see what looked like a barn in the far distance to the east. Most likely a farm, then. Maybe Peter could ask for assistance there. All he had to do was follow the line of dark-brown wooden fence interspersed with metal netting, and hopefully it would lead him to the main entrance.

Having made a decision, Peter grabbed his satchel, locked the car, and began walking. The crunch of the soles of his custom leather boots on the cobblestone sidewalk was the only sound that echoed in the air as the vibrant scent of wildflowers filled his nostrils.

He took a deep breath, catching a whiff of citrus and rose. The fresh air freed up his lungs, and Peter wished he could just bottle it up and take it back home. This was what he missed while living and working in a city like New York.

Soon, he spotted the entrance of the farm—a large wrought-iron arch upheld by two stalwart stone pillars. As he approached, the gate swung open. Must be sensor controlled, he thought. Peter looked up and at first didn't see any obvious security cameras, but then noticed what looked like one embedded in the top section of the wrought-iron arch. Nice, he thought, impressed. Maybe this place wasn't an average farm like he'd expected.

Peter walked through the open gates and followed a long fenced-in concrete driveway that soon transitioned into cobblestone as he approached a massive log-and-stone house set in the midst of a sprawling manicured lawn with the majestic mountains as a backdrop. The place looked positively enchanting, and Peter hoped the owners were as welcoming as the setting.

As he neared the house, the front door jerked open, and a black shape flew out in his direction.

Peter jumped to the left to avoid the oncoming onslaught, but his efforts failed.

And that was how he ended up on the ground, mired with horse dung, staring up into the last face he'd ever expected to see.

CHAPTER 3

Maggie Fields wiped the surface of the commercial-grade range one more time. The smell of freshly baked cookies and apple chips still lingered in the air.

"Are you sure you'll be okay alone?" Max Dexin asked in a concerned tone. He was going on vacation, and Maggie would be alone in the big house.

Maggie turned and gave her foster son an encouraging smile. Most people still thought she was his housekeeper like Maggie used to say, but Max and his brothers had been Maggie's legal wards after their mom passed away until they came of age. "I'll be fine," she insisted.

This was the first time in a long time that the ranch was going to be minimally staffed, and Max was rightfully worried. Dexin Ranch was a small working ranch operation that raised show horses and cattle. The summer was usually a busy season for horse shows, so most of the ranch hands and one of Max's brothers had been pulled from their duties to take the horses to two different large shows in two states. A junior ranch hand remained to handle any immediate needs of the animals left behind on the ranch.

Dex, the other brother responsible for the ranch operations, was supposed to have stayed back on the ranch during Max's vacation, but he had headed out early this morning to grab some emergency supplies for the ranch and was expected to be back the next day. Maggie could handle any problems in the meantime—she'd helped run the ranch for many years before the boys took over. She'd been looking forward to a quiet day like this for a while, and nothing could deter her. Maggie could take care of herself just fine.

"Are you sure?" Max asked again.

"I'll be okay." She placed her hands on her hips and pretended to glare at him, even though he towered over her five-foot-six figure. "Are you saying I can't take care of myself, cowboy?"

Max lifted his hands in mock surrender and took

a few steps back. "Sorry, ma'am," he replied with a chuckle.

"You got that right." Then Maggie's face softened into a smile. "Truly, I'll be alright. You, however, need to go—you can't keep Becca and Chloe waiting in the car. Make sure you take the time to rest and forget about work on this trip. You've been too busy these past few months getting the ER Center set up while still working at that Dexington hospital, and Becca and Chloe need this time with you. Besides, I need more young'uns running around in this big old house, and that's not going to happen by itself." Becca was Max's wife, and Chloe his four-year-old child. They'd only been reunited with Max a couple of months ago. A series of events had kept Max and Becca apart for five years, during which time Becca had been forced to raise Chloe on her own. It was only through the Lord's providence that they'd found each other again.

"Yes, ma'am." Maggie chuckled as Max's ears turned a bright red.

She waved him away with her hands. "Okay, go before Chloe finds another reason to come back for an extra cookie. You know how hard it is to say no to her once she's made up her mind."

"Thanks for the cookies and chips," Max said, raising the large storage bags he held in one hand.

Maggie had baked those cookies and chips early this morning for them to take on their trip, as they were Chloe's favorites.

"Anytime. Now shoo!"

Max leaned forward and gave Maggie a warm hug. "I'll see you in a few days."

Maggie watched as Max left the kitchen and made his way through the adjoining living area and out the front door. The sound of a vehicle starting and then rolling down the driveway filled the air before it faded away. Max had always been a wonderful and caring man, but meeting Becca again had settled him. Maggie had never seen him so happy as when he was a husband and a father.

A long-buried ache rose in her heart, but Maggie stamped it down. She was looking forward to a day of peace and quiet, not one tainted by painful memories best left forgotten. Memories of a time when she'd looked forward to marriage and kids—a dream that had been destroyed. She'd had a hard time opening her heart again to love after losing a certain young blue-eyed man she'd loved with all her heart, and then at some point she'd stopped trying.

A chance meeting with Max's mom—a young widow working hard to raise four boys—had been the balm her soul needed, and Maggie had stepped in to help and then continued watching over the boys after their mom died. The rest was history. Her life had ended up more wonderful than Maggie would have ever imagined, and it had been more than enough.

Until recently, after watching how happy Max was with his new family.

Now, thoughts about the young man and what might have been invaded her mind now and again when least expected.

Maggie shook her head. Thinking about him was borrowing trouble. It was too late—she'd heard he'd married, and he probably had grown kids of his own by now. Besides, everything had worked out for the best—she'd found out she was a rancher at heart, something that would never have worked with him, since his life had been set on the prestigious path dictated by his family. Any memories of him had to stay in the past where they rightfully belonged. There was no point in letting it ruin what was supposed to be a wonderful day.

Maggie was planning to relax at her favorite spot near an old red barn on the ranch and listen to the sound of the nearby stream gurgling away while reading her new historical novel, which had just arrived this morning. She'd been anticipating its release forever and couldn't wait to dig in.

"Ouch!" Something bumped against her legs, and Maggie looked down to see what it was. Ornie, one of the ranch's baby goats, stared up at her for a moment before scurrying away.

"Hey! Where do you think you're going?" Ornie wasn't allowed in the main house, but Chloe must have let him in. She'd claimed him as her pet and spoiled him, and that seemed to have emboldened Ornie, who now loved to run around the house whenever Chloe managed to sneak him in. Maggie loved him, but she hated cleaning up the random poop he loved to drop around. She had to get him out before she was forced to start cleaning the house all over again.

"Ornie, come back here!" Maggie dropped the towel she'd been holding, grabbed an oatmeal cookie from its jar on the kitchen counter, and hurried after him as he made a dash down the hallway that led to Max's section of the house. She would get him out of the house no matter what it took. If Ornie thought he was the stubbornest creature in the house, he had another think coming.

No one, not even Ornie, could disrupt Maggie's plans for today.

CHAPTER 4

*M*aggie threw the cookie into the air even as she jerked the front door open. She didn't necessarily need Ornie in his pen—Clive, the ranch hand, would take care of it. She just needed to get him out of the house, and nothing worked like the oatmeal or apricot cookies Ornie loved, which was why Maggie always made sure she had some on hand.

Ornie jumped into the air and out the door to grab the cookie she'd tossed. *Yes!* She made to close the door.

"Aargh!" a distinct, strangely familiar, masculine voice cried out.

Maggie's head spun back as if in whiplash, and she rushed out of the house. She'd had no idea someone was at the door. She found a tall, lean man sprawled on the driveway. Ornie, on the other hand, sauntered away, unconcerned, from where he lay.

Maggie's hand covered her mouth, and she rushed to the stranger. Ornie must have collided with him! "Oh my goodness! Are you alright?"

The man cut a dashing figure—even though he was on the ground—dressed in a white button-down shirt tucked into fitted jeans and long legs that seemed to extend for miles ending in a pair of chestnut-brown wingtip dress boots. He had a lean build that was only possible if he exercised or was involved in some outdoor activity regularly. His profile looked somewhat familiar, but his face was turned from Maggie as he stared at Ornie skittering away.

That was when Maggie noticed he was sitting on horse dung. *Oh no!* She'd totally forgotten about the poop Bella, Max's favorite horse, had dropped on their way back to the horse barn after Maggie had taken her out for a ride this morning. She'd planned to take care of it, but it had totally slipped her mind with helping Chloe and Becca get ready for their trip. Max must have missed it too.

But more importantly, she hoped he wasn't injured. "Are you okay?" she asked again.

The man's face swung back to her.

Maggie suddenly couldn't breathe. She'd recognize those blue eyes anywhere. It was like all the air in her lungs had chosen to desert her when she needed it most. *It can't be real,* her mind thought over and over again as she forced herself to take a deep breath.

How was it possible? How could Peter Taylor be here in front of her home?

Her heart thumped so loudly that Maggie placed a hand over her chest as if to quieten it. She suddenly felt dizzy, but she shook her head to drive away the fog that threatened to overcome her.

It couldn't be *him.* Maybe it was someone that looked like him—a doppelgänger or a distant relative of his she'd never met. Because there was no way Peter Taylor could be here in front of her.

"Mae?" he asked in a disbelieving tone.

Oh my goodness. It was really him. Peter was the only one who'd called her by that nickname. She'd wondered over the years whether she'd see him again, and now here he was, staring up at her.

But the past was over and had to stay that way. She had to keep her heart safe. *Take a deep breath, Maggie. You can do this.*

"Are you injured?" she asked with a false confidence that masked how anxious she was.

Maggie could see his eyes still appeared dazed. He shook his head slightly. "I don't think so."

"Here, grab my hand. I'll help you up," she said as she extended her hand to him.

He reached for her, and she forced herself not to flinch from the electricity that crackled between them when their hands touched. He must have felt it too because he jerked backward and ended up further mired in the horse dung.

"Ugh!" he said, looking down at his jeans stained with horse poop.

Maggie couldn't help the laughter that bubbled up from within her. He looked awful and yet cute at the same time.

"Hey! You shouldn't laugh," he said, which just made Maggie laugh more. The tension in her body eased away too.

"Okay, okay. I'm sorry," she said with a chuckle. "Let's try again."

She managed to help him stand up again and then jumped back once she was done. Peter cocked his eyebrow at her. "Just trying to avoid the horse poop," she said. She couldn't help the grin that split across her face.

His lips curled into the familiar smile she'd always loved, and Maggie felt her heart twist in pain as she remembered the moments when it'd once made her heart skip a beat, like it did now. Her smile disappeared.

"Mae—"

She turned away from him. "Why don't I help you get changed into clean clothes? Then you can tell me what you're doing here."

CHAPTER 5

*P*eter still couldn't believe Maggie Fields was right here in front of him. How was it possible? Even though she was older, she looked even more beautiful in a pink flowery blouse that accentuated her glowing skin, and a pair of skinny jeans that fit her to a tee. Maggie had always been put together without meaning to, and it appeared that hadn't changed over the years.

But mixed emotions swelled up in him. She had broken his heart after all. Then why did he feel a flicker of happiness light up in his chest just by seeing her again?

Maggie didn't wait for his response and instead led the way to a smaller entrance at the side of the house. Peter had no choice but to grab his satchel—

which had managed to remain in one piece—from where it had fallen and follow her, though his mind whirled with questions.

He passed through the side door entrance into a small room with rows of worn boots lined up on the lower shelves and jackets and raincoats hanging in rows on higher racks. Still, every piece in the room looked like it had been placed there with intention.

A pang of jealousy flashed through him. Maybe the shoes belonged to her husband. Who was the lucky fellow, and had Maggie met him before or after she broke Peter's heart? Wait! Was he part of the Boston social circle, the same one Maggie and Peter had grown up in? Probably not—Peter couldn't recall any of his peers being interested in farming, and he would have heard about the wedding.

Instead, Maggie had disappeared after she'd broken his heart, and all news about her had dried up. He could have gone after her, but she'd insisted he didn't, and he had respected her wishes. But he'd regretted keeping that promise every minute of the two years he'd mourned her absence in his life.

"This is the mudroom," Maggie said without turning back. Then she motioned to a door on the far wall. "That leads to the bathroom. You can take a shower if you'd prefer. I'll grab a change of clothes for you, which I'll place on that bench close to the door. You might want to leave your boots there too. I'll clean them up for you while you shower. Just drop your clothes in the laundry basket in the bathroom, and I'll pick them up once you're done. Everything else you need is in there." She turned to leave the room without making eye contact with him.

"Thank you," he replied. "Mae—"

"It's Maggie. We'll talk later once you're done," she replied, and then she left the room.

Peter had so many questions he wanted to ask her, but he figured the faster he cleaned up, the earlier he'd have a chance to do so. He tucked his sunglasses into his satchel, dropped it on the bench, and then carefully removed his boots and placed them beneath it. Then he headed into the bathroom.

The bathroom was steeped in understated luxury, with brick walls in subtle shades of warm brown, which matched its beige marble floor tiles. A dark wooden vanity with antique-brass sink fixtures—and a drawer that contained all the toiletries he'd ever need—sat against one wall and beside a towel rack with multiple rolled towels and opposite a huge shower area with tiles that matched the flooring. A large oval distressed mirror hung above the sink, completing the picture.

Nice. A part of him was relieved things had turned out well for her in the end, though another part wished he'd been the one to provide such things for her. But then he remembered why he hadn't had the chance to do so.

He shook his head. What was he thinking? It was all in the past. Besides, Maggie was now a married woman, and he had no business dwelling on such thoughts. She had to be waiting for him to finish, so the sooner he hurried through the shower, the better.

Ten minutes later, Peter was done showering, had dried his hair, and had changed into the blue button-down shirt and jeans that Maggie had left for him on the bench outside the bathroom door. Surprisingly, the clothes were a good fit. Peter wondered if her husband was the original owner of the clothes. He donned his shoes, picked up his satchel, and stepped out of the mudroom into the main living area.

Peter looked around with the practiced eye of someone who recognized superior workmanship when he saw it. The house had definitely seen the touch of a talented interior designer. Logs and stone were interwoven to create a look that was rugged and rustic, yet still modern. The overall tone was warm and inviting, and Peter could see why anyone would want to stay here and never leave.

Maggie was sitting on the large couch in the area and got up as soon as Peter approached. "Feel free to sit down," she said, motioning to the array of seats in the living room. "I'll be right back." She headed toward the mudroom, and he assumed that she'd gone to take care of his clothes. She was back five minutes later, now wearing a pair of cowboy boots. "Your clothes are in the washer, and it should take about an hour to an hour-and-a-half for them to be ready," she said.

So he was stuck here for the next hour and a half. "Thank you for doing this," he replied.

She acknowledged it with a nod. "I hope you don't mind, but I need to go check on the horses. Why don't you wait for me here? It won't take me long, and I'll be right back."

As comfy as the couch in front of him looked, Peter would rather be where he could see Maggie. It still felt like a dream that she was speaking to him. "Why don't I come with you instead?"

"Sure, if you want."

Maggie turned and led the way out of the house. After a few steps, she veered left and headed toward what looked like a horse barn with sliding doors. One half of the doors was propped open by a wheelbarrow held in place with a solid cement block.

"Be careful about that," Maggie said as she side-stepped the wheelbarrow and entered the barn. Peter glanced at the makeshift prop but said nothing as he followed her into the space.

The barn was large and airy with a wide aisle framed by multiple horse stalls on either side, what looked like a tack room at the back, and a second-floor hayloft. Each horse stall gate boasted the hinged European door style with a wooden lower section framed by steel and a V-necked upper section, also made out of steel. The interior looked newly constructed. The smell of sweaty leather, fresh pine shavings, and the sweet scent of hay lingered in the air.

Most of the horse stalls were empty as Maggie led Peter down the cobblestoned aisle all the way to the last stall where a beautiful dark thoroughbred mare rose from where she'd lain and ambled to the stall door.

"Hello, Bella," Maggie said in a warm voice as she reached out and rubbed the horse's neck. Bella nuzzled her nose against the front pocket of Maggie's shirt in response.

Maggie chuckled. "Smart girl." The sound of her laughter touched a part of Peter's soul that had seemed dead for a while now, and he fought to suppress it. "So you're looking for some treats?" Peter watched as Maggie pulled out a small paper bag from her jean pocket, laid some baby carrots flat on her hand, and offered them to the horse, who quickly chomped them down. "Good girl," Maggie said. "You like that, don't you?" She looked into the stall. "And it seems Clive has been here to see you, right?" she said to Bella as she continued rubbing her neck.

"Who's Clive?" Peter couldn't help asking.

"The ranch hand," Maggie answered without looking at him.

The air was awkward, but not uncomfortable. There was so much to ask, and Peter didn't know where to begin. He was supposed to be on his way to see his mentor, but now he wondered if meeting Maggie was the real reason his car had broken down —the actual purpose for which he'd set out on the journey today.

"I didn't expect to meet you here, Maggie," he started. He couldn't read the expression on her face, so he just hurried on. "But I'm happy we met."

"How did you know where I lived?" she asked softly.

"I didn't."

She looked at him in surprise. "What do you mean?"

Maggie would probably think his story was ridiculous. "My car broke down not far from the entrance of your farm."

"It's not a farm. It's a ranch."

"Oh. Sorry about that."

"You wouldn't have known. Your car broke down?"

"Yes. I was on my way to see a friend who lives about two hours away from here when the car suddenly stopped. Unfortunately, I couldn't connect to roadside assistance, so I figured I might find some help here." From the way she stared at him, he couldn't tell if she believed him.

Finally she looked away. "The network in the area is spotty at best, but we have our own cell tower," she said. "It's only available if your phone is connected to our network. Let me call the local mechanic for you. He can pretty much handle any car."

"I'd appreciate that."

She stepped away from Bella, pulled out her phone, and moved a couple more steps away to make the call. Soon, she was back. "He's away at a client's house but should be here in about forty-five minutes. Hope that works."

"Sure." It wasn't like he was going anywhere until his clothes were ready.

Then Maggie seemed to be staring at something beyond him. "Ornie!" she exclaimed.

Peter turned to see the baby goat from before, standing a few steps away in the middle of the aisle. Before he could even respond, Maggie had already started marching in the goat's direction. "Ornie, shoo!" she said.

Ornie turned and scampered toward the barn entrance. Peter stood and watched him go. There was no way he was getting entangled with that goat. One tumble in horse dung was more than enough. He observed with amusement as Maggie chased after him, then watched in horror as Ornie jumped on the wheelbarrow, which tumbled over and crashed on the floor. Ornie flew into the air and then out the door. But the wheelbarrow no longer held the door open, and it began to slide closed.

"Oh, no!" Maggie screamed and reached out her arm to block it from sealing shut.

"Mae, watch out!" Peter shouted as he raced to the entrance. He might not have been a rancher, but he'd ridden horses growing up and still played the occasional polo match. Peter had been around horse stalls enough to know there was no way Maggie could keep it open. Instead, her arm would be trapped and crushed in the process.

Peter reached her in time to pull her into his arms just as the door closed. A familiar spark of electricity coursed through his skin as they made contact. A warm cinnamon and spice scent enveloped him, triggering his buried feelings. Emotions he'd locked tight in his heart and never thought would see the light of day again—feelings that had no business being in his life again—all came flooding back.

Maggie pushed him away. "What do you think you're doing?" she hissed.

He felt a heavy loss as she exited his arms, but he managed to keep his face neutral. "Saving your life."

Her eyes sparked with fire as she pointed at the door. "I could have stopped it from closing."

Peter shook his head. Even one of those steel sliding doors could incur serious damage. "You could have hurt yourself and broken your bones," he said. "That door weighs a ton." He waited for her to calm down and knew the moment when the implication of what he'd said sank in as her face paled. "What about the emergency exit?" he asked.

But she rallied quickly. "It's stuck," Maggie said as she placed her hands on her hips. "This barn was reconstructed after a fire burned it down a few months ago— the only thing left to replace are the doors," she said.

"All the horses have been staying in another barn, but Bella and her friends were moved here today to make it easier for me to check on them in the next twenty-four hours." She looked confident and fiery, and Peter was sure her mind was already racing for a solution.

His heart stirred. Gosh, she still had that spark, the one that had made him fall in love with her many years ago. He was in deep trouble, especially since he had no right to be feeling this way about her. He really had to focus on the current situation if he wanted to leave this place unscathed. "So what do we do now?" he asked. "Are we trapped here?"

"It's a good thing that door can be opened from the outside. Let me make a call. Clive is somewhere on the property and can come and open it for us." Maggie pulled out her phone, dialed a number, and waited a few seconds as she held the phone against her ear. "He's not picking up. Maybe he's with the cattle. I'll just leave him a message." She stayed silent for another few seconds before speaking. "Hey, Clive, this is Maggie. I'm stuck in the main horse barn. Could you come and open the door as soon as you get this message? Thanks." She ended the call and turned back to Peter. "I'm sure he'll be here soon. Why don't you sit on one of those benches over there? I'll finish taking care of these horses, and then we can talk."

"Can I help?" he asked.

"No, it's fine. It will only take me a few minutes. It seems Clive has already fed them and cleaned out their stalls."

Peter dropped his satchel beside him and watched as Maggie stopped by each horse, fed them treats, examined their stalls, and massaged their necks. Then she entered the tack room—most likely to wash her hands—before returning to sit on the opposite bench.

The awkward air between them returned. If Peter wasn't careful, it would continue this way until he left. There had to be a reason why he'd met Maggie again at this time, and maybe the best place to start was to ask about the one thing he'd always wanted to know. Time to take the bull by the horns. It was either now or never.

"Why did you really leave me at the altar, Mae?"

CHAPTER 6

aggie froze, and her heart skipped a beat. This was the one question she'd dreaded over the years, and now Peter had asked it.

No one knew the real reason why she'd done it. She'd kept it buried deep in her heart for all this time and had planned for it to stay there forever. Now he wanted it out, and once spoken, it would never be hidden again.

But did it really matter anymore? There could never be anything between Peter and her again, so maybe it was a moot point. And maybe a little part of her wanted the misunderstanding between them to end.

She fiddled with the phone in her hand and then

looked up at him. "Your mother threatened me," she said.

Peter blanched, all the color leaving his face. Maggie felt sorry for him—it was probably the last thing he'd expected to hear.

But there was still more.

"She hated me after my parents died and left me with nothing." Maggie gave a harsh laugh as she remembered the venom Peter's mom had spewed. "My marriage to you was supposed to have been the best investment she'd made, but my parents losing their company and then dying meant I was suddenly a pariah. I was no longer good enough for her golden child."

All the emotions from that fateful day came flooding back like it had happened yesterday, and Maggie drew in a tremulous breath to calm herself. "Your mother promised she would do everything to ruin me, even go so far as to make sure I got expelled from Wellesley if that was what it took. From the fury in her eyes, I knew she meant it too. I'd just lost everything in my life, and she was threatening to take away the one thing I had left. So even though I knew you would have fought for me, I also realized you'd never win against her. No one had ever been able to."

Peter collapsed against the wall like all the

strength had deserted his body. Maggie felt bad for crushing the image he had of his mother, but he'd asked for the truth. The truth wasn't always sweet or beautiful. It could leave a taste so bitter it tainted everything else one consumed.

"I didn't know," he said in a quiet voice.

"How could you? I didn't know either till I was in that position."

"Why didn't you tell me?"

"It would have torn you both apart. I knew what it was like to lose my mother. It would have crushed you, considering how close you two were. I couldn't do that to you."

"But your leaving me destroyed me." Maggie looked at his face and glimpsed the devastation written all over it. The ache in her heart grew, and she wrapped her arms around herself as if to soothe it. She'd known she'd hurt him, but not like this. "You meant everything to me, Mae, and I would have fought for you with all I had." His blue eyes held hers, and Maggie had to look away to keep from drowning in the sorrow in them. "But you didn't even give me a chance. You knew I didn't care about the wealth and the lavish lifestyle. That was part of what drew us together. I already had an inheritance from my grandfather which would have been more than enough to support us until I finished medical school and started working.

"But, you didn't trust me. You left me standing at the altar, Mae. Remember all the dreams we had and how excited we were about them? Everything got shattered, just like that. My whole world collapsed." Peter rubbed his hands over his face. "I still don't know how I survived the next two years after that. I have no memory of what I did during that time." He took a deep breath as if to steady himself. "You broke me, Mae."

Tears rose unbidden at the back of Maggie's eyelids, and she fought to keep them from falling. She wished she could wrap her arms around him and soothe the hurt away, but it was too late now. Everything was gone, and only the ashes of regrets remained.

"I'm sorry," was all she could say. "I'm so sorry, Peter."

CHAPTER 7

A pregnant silence prevailed as Peter fought to regain his composure. He'd had no idea his mother had been behind Maggie's departure from his life, and he felt a strong sense of betrayal. How could she have done this to him, knowing how much Maggie meant to him?

It was all his fault. He should have guessed what happened, especially when his mother hadn't made a fuss about Maggie's disappearance. That should have been the first clue. Instead, he'd assumed at the time that she was just being her usual stoic self.

His shoulders deflated. But what did it matter now? She was as far away from him as the heavens were from the earth. No matter how he still felt about her, it was just too late.

His eyes landed on Maggie's hands.

Or was it?

Maggie was wearing a Wellesley class ring on her right fourth finger, yet she had no band on her left ring finger. That was strange. From what he'd seen over the years, women who liked rings enough to put them on would also wear a wedding ring, if they had one.

Hope flared in his chest, and his heart beat a little faster. Could it be? "Maggie," he said carefully, "what about your husband?"

Maggie's eyes widened in surprise before her face closed off. Then she straightened her shoulders. "Why do you ask?" she said. "Do you think I couldn't work hard and manage all this by myself?"

"Not at all," Peter hurried to reassure her. "You, of all people, have always been able to achieve anything you set your mind to. I just wondered since this ranch seems so big. I remember you always loved cozy places."

She stared at him for a moment with those beautiful eyes of hers that stirred his soul. "I'm not married," she said finally.

He'd hoped, yet her response took him by surprise. "He passed away?"

Maggie let out a sigh as if frustrated. "I've never married."

Peter couldn't help the feeling of exhilaration that leapt up in his heart. It spread throughout his body, livening it up so much that he wanted to scream for joy from the rooftop. He still had a chance! Maybe it was the Lord that had led him to this place. Even though it seemed crazy and farfetched and wild, like he was on a train that had lost its brakes, maybe this was his second chance—an opportunity to live the life he'd always imagined with Maggie. But he needed to know more about how she lived, and how he might possibly fit in—

"I live with my foster sons," she responded as if hearing the question in his heart. "They run the ranch."

Sons, which meant more than one. Peter wondered what the story behind it was, since she'd never married, but he didn't ask. It didn't matter—he had his own children too. Sons, she'd said. He could win sons over. But first, he had to convince Maggie to give this maddening possibility a chance.

Meeting Maggie again, realizing he still had feelings for her, finding out she wasn't married—it might have seemed everything was happening so fast, but maybe it was time to take a leap of faith, a chance to find the pot of gold at the end of the rainbow. But he had to tread carefully so as not to frighten her away.

"Mae," he said softly, "what if there's still a chance for us?"

CHAPTER 8

Maggie jumped up so fast Peter was afraid the bench would flip over. She pointed an accusing finger at Peter. "I may be single, but I'm not stupid. How dare you?"

Peter got up as well and took a step toward her. "Look, it's not what you think."

Maggie's face grew furious. "Don't come near me. I'll call the cops if you do."

"Mae, I'm single too."

Maggie shook her head in disbelief. "You can't fool me. I heard about your wedding. How could you insult me by even thinking we could have an affair? You must really think low of me."

Peter had to get through to her, to convince her to

give them a chance. "I lost my wife sixteen years ago. I'm really single."

She gestured at his hand. "You're still wearing a wedding band."

Peter looked down at the gold band on his finger. It had been a part of him for so long that he'd forgotten about it. "It's a force of habit, and it has helped keep interested women at bay. I haven't wanted another relationship since my wife passed away. Until now. Until you."

But Maggie refused to budge. "Prove it."

Peter threw up his hands in the air. "How?"

"That's up to you. But you better not move one more step in my direction until you do."

Peter let out a sigh and rubbed the back of his neck. How was he going to get himself out of this mess? His mind raced as he searched for a solution. Then an idea occurred to him. He picked up his satchel and began to rummage through it.

"What are you doing?" Maggie asked.

"Looking for my phone."

"Why?"

"You'll see. Give me a second." Peter scrolled through his phone till he found what he was looking for. "Here, take a look." He extended the phone to Maggie.

Maggie stared at the phone like it was a viper. "What is it?"

"Look at it and you'll see."

Maggie grudgingly accepted the phone. Peter watched as she studied what was on the screen. He knew the instant she read the truth—her eyes widened, and he thought he saw a glimpse of hope in her eyes.

Thank you, God, and thank you, Greg. Gregory Hamilton, his colleague at the hospital, had forwarded him a snapshot of a magazine feature about Peter after he'd won the excellence award. The reporter had mentioned that Peter was single and an eligible bachelor. Peter had dismissed the news, but was now grateful he hadn't deleted it. There was no way Maggie would think he'd made it up on the fly. "So?" he asked.

"What do you mean?"

"Will you go out with me, Mae?"

Her cheeks flushed red, but Maggie ignored it and handed his phone back to him. "It can't work."

Peter's heart sank. "What do you mean?"

"One, it has been too many years. We've both changed and are no longer the people we used to be. We're practically strangers. Two, I love my ranch life, Peter."

Peter refused to give up. "We can get to know each other again. And who says I'm not interested in a life on the ranch? That's why I'm asking you out, Mae, instead of asking you to marry me." A thought crossed his mind. "Or would you prefer to marry me instead?"

The blush on her cheeks spread all over her face and her neck. "Peter!"

"I mean it, Mae. Option one or option two works for me."

Maggie shook her head. "You're mad."

Peter took a step toward her and watched her reaction. She didn't say anything. He took another step. "I think God is giving us a second chance, and I don't want to miss it again," he said. "I still feel something for you, and the way you reacted earlier told me you do too."

"No, I don't," she insisted.

He took another step till he was standing in front of her. "Are you sure about that?"

"I'm sure."

"Prove it." Peter placed a hand on her cheek, and he heard her breath hitch. *Liar.* He held her gaze, and she didn't look away—her warm expressive eyes digging deep into his soul. So Peter laid it bare, exposing all the love for her to see, and hoping she'd accept it.

His skin hummed at the excitement of kissing her. Instead, Peter traced the curve of her face, memorizing every line, freckle, and age spot, the evidence of her wisdom and grace—elements that were uniquely hers and which only enhanced who she'd become—imprinting them in his heart. It didn't matter that she was no longer young—she was still as beautiful as ever, and she stole his breath away.

He leaned forward till their breaths intermingled. Her cinnamon and spice scent enveloped him and sent every fiber of his being into overdrive.

His eyes searched hers. "Can I kiss you?" he asked. Maggie said nothing but didn't move away, which Peter took as consent and lowered his lips to hers.

The kiss was light, gentle, to let her know he remembered her, that she had been his world, and that she mattered to him. Kissing her was like coming home after being on a long circuitous journey, and he sighed with pleasure.

Then he felt her arms loop around his neck, and that was all the permission he needed. Peter drew her closer and deepened the kiss. Suddenly, it was like they were the only ones that existed, finally mourning together the loss of the love they'd lost years ago and replacing it with the promise of a future together, a delicate flowering love born anew—one that was here to stay and which would survive, despite their differences and who they'd become.

All too soon, Peter ended the kiss and held her close in his arms, resting his cheek against hers. They still fit together, even better than they had so many years ago. "I've missed you," he said.

"I've missed us," Maggie responded quietly.

"So will you marry me?" he asked.

Maggie laughed. "You're crazy, Peter."

The corners of his lips curled into a smile. "But I'm crazier about you."

She pulled away yet remained in his arms. "You don't even know me. At least not anymore."

He tipped her chin upward and looked into those eyes that showed her fear and uncertainty. "I know you. You may have so many more layers now, but at your core you're still the same Mae I fell in love with over thirty years ago. I look forward to discovering all your layers."

But she wasn't convinced. "It won't work, Peter. What about your family? What about the dragon lady?"

Peter's face wrinkled in confusion. "Dragon who?"

"Your mother. She's still alive, isn't she? She won't stand for this."

The corners of Peter's eyes wrinkled in fiery determination. "Do you want to find out? Say you'll marry me, and I'll show you."

"Peter—"

"Please say you'll marry me. It doesn't have to be today."

"Okay."

"Good." He picked up his phone, dialed a number, and placed it on speaker mode. "Hello, Mother."

"Are you crazy, Peter?" Maggie whispered. Peter put a finger over his mouth to quiet her.

"Peter, is everything alright?" his mother said from the other end of the line.

"I'm getting married, Mother. Just thought you should know."

"What?" his mother shrieked. Maggie tried to reach for the phone to end the call, but Peter held her away.

"It's not a joke," he said.

"Are you trying to give me a heart attack?"

"I'm marrying someone I've loved for a very long time. Someone you know."

"Don't tell me … Margaret?"

"Yes, Mother. I have to go. I thought you should know."

"Peter, wait! I will not allow it. Not her. She's your past."

"It doesn't matter, Mother. She's my future too. I will marry her, and no one can stop me this time around. Not even you."

"What do you mean?" Peter thought he heard a slight tremor in her voice.

"I know everything now, Mother."

He heard a sharp inhale from the other end of the line. "Peter, you're making a mistake," his mother said as she tried to recover.

"I'm doing the best thing for me. I love you, Mother, and I hope you'll come to my wedding."

"Peter, wait—"

"Goodbye, Mother. I'll talk to you later." He ended the call. "Wonderful." Then he turned to Maggie. "Everything is going to be alright," he said as he wrapped her into a hug.

Maggie rested her head against his chest. "I don't know. Everything is moving so fast, like a roller coaster."

"I thought it might be better to tear off the band-aid quickly so that she can start getting used to the idea." He held Maggie away and looked into her eyes. "But I will marry you no matter what she says." Peter gave her a warm smile. "I'm more than old enough to make that decision on my own. But it doesn't have to be today. We'll go at our own pace and take as much time as we need to get to know each other again, okay?"

Maggie gave him a small smile. "Okay."

Peter led her back to the bench and sat beside her.

His phone rang at that moment, and he looked at the screen. "It's my friend and mentor I was going to see. I'll put him on speakerphone." He swiped the answer button. "Hey, old man."

"Who are you calling old man?" a gravelly voice responded. "Have you looked in the mirror lately?" Peter chuckled. "When are you getting here? I'm sure all the fish have taken off by now."

"I won't be able to make it," Peter said.

"What's wrong? Is everything alright?"

"I have important business to take care of."

"Why do you sound so chirpy?" his mentor asked in a suspicious tone. "Wait a minute! It's a woman, isn't it?"

"I'm getting married."

The guy swore under his breath. "Are you kidding me? Are you having some sort of midlife crisis?"

"I'm as serious as that Viagra you've been taking."

Peter heard what sounded like someone choking. "Are you trying to kill me? Now I've spilled water all over the front of my pants!"

"I have to go. I'll talk to you later, Horatio."

"Hey! How can you throw out a bomb like that and just leave me hanging? Who's the lucky woman?"

"Bye, old man." Peter ended the call.

"You're nuts," Maggie said. "I can't believe you told him."

"He would have been on my case if I didn't tell him the truth. Don't worry. He's more like a big brother to me, and he'll keep it a secret till he's sure I've told everyone. I don't plan on telling anyone else till you give me the green light, and you can be certain my mother will keep her lips sealed for now. I doubt she'd want the rumor mills in Boston to work overtime on her behalf."

"Promise?"

"Promise." Peter drew Maggie close and gave her a kiss on the forehead. "You're worth everything to me, and I don't want to lose you again." He placed his forehead against hers. "I'm afraid to lose you again," he said in a softer tone. "Are you scared?"

She snuggled deeper into him. "I'm not scared as long as we take it slow. It has been a long time."

"Okay."

"Now kiss me again."

"Happy to oblige, ma'am." Then Peter leaned forward and kissed her. It was a tender kiss that unraveled him as she responded with equal fervor—a kiss of new beginnings, longing, hope, and sweetness all wrapped into one, and he never wanted it to end.

"Maggie, what's going on here?" a voice boomed out.

CHAPTER 9

The sound of the voice brought reality crashing back in, and Maggie jerked away from Peter and onto her feet. Peter got up as well.

Oh my goodness, Maggie thought. This couldn't be happening. It was too early for him, for them to find out about the relationship. She'd planned to ease them into it. But now the cat was out of the bag.

Take a deep breath, Maggie. You can do this.

Maggie turned toward the man who'd made his way down the aisle in giant strides, but she reached for Peter's hand and held it in hers. If he was the same Peter she'd known, deep down he still needed that reassurance that they were in this together, no matter how confident he'd sounded.

"Hello, Dex," Maggie said with a smile. "I didn't know you'd be back today."

Dex looked from Maggie to Peter. "Who the hell is he?"

"Dex Dexin, you are not too old for me to wash your mouth with soap," she countered in a steely voice.

Dex managed to look contrite. "Yes, ma'am. I'm sorry." He ran his hand through his hair and sighed. "This wasn't what I was expecting to see, that's all. I saw the barn door shut, figured something was wrong, and came here right away."

Maggie placed a hand on his arm. "Thanks for caring." She squeezed it and then let go. "Peter Taylor, meet Dex Dexin, one of my foster sons. Dex, meet Peter, my boyfriend."

Dex's eyes grew so round Maggie thought they'd pop out of his head. "Boyfriend? Since when?"

"Since today," Peter responded. He extended his free hand to Dex. "It's nice to meet you."

Dex ignored the hand and instead studied Peter like he was a shark. "How come this is the first time I'm hearing about you?"

"Peter and I have known each other for a very, very long time," Maggie said matter-of-factly. Then her tone softened. "I really like him, and I hope you'll give him a chance."

Dex ran his free hand through his dark hair. "This is such a big surprise."

"Can you try?"

"I'll try, but baby steps, okay? You have to understand, this is a huge shock. Do Max and Jax know?" Jax was another one of Max's brothers, the one that had traveled for the horse show.

Maggie shook her head. "No."

"Okay, let's hold off on telling them till they come back. I don't want Max to turn the jet around, or Jax to leave the show and hop on the next plane."

Maggie chuckled. The boys were crazy enough to do that. "Sounds good to me."

Dex turned to Peter. "I can't really say it was nice meeting you, but I trust Maggie's judgment, so I hope to get to know you better. Fair?" He extended his hand.

"That works for me," Peter said with a smile as he accepted the handshake.

"Okay, I'll leave you lovebirds to it. I'm exhausted, and I need to take a shower."

"Dex!" Maggie protested. He grinned in response. "Did you get everything you wanted to buy?"

"Yes, I did. And quickly too. The Lord must have known I needed to come back and catch you guys like this."

"Dex!"

"I need to call the door guys now that we have everything to fix this barn door. We can't have strange things going on here like I just saw," he teased.

Maggie's ears grew warm. If he was younger, she would have cuffed the back of his head. But she deserved it. The good Lord knew she'd teased the boys a lot over the years. It was payback time, it seemed.

Dex laughed. "Talk to you later, Maggie. Peter." He turned and left the barn.

Maggie shook her head in disbelief and slumped back on the bench. "This is moving much faster than I expected. It's all your fault, you know."

Peter sat beside her. "Maybe it's the Lord's speed."

"So, now it's God's fault, eh?"

Peter kept a solemn face. "The Lord's timing is the best. All we have to do is go with the flow."

Maggie smacked his arm. "Since when did you become so honey-mouthed?"

Peter grinned. "It comes with age and wisdom, darling."

Maggie stared at Peter for a moment and then burst out laughing. She had a feeling that the current Peter was definitely more interesting than the old one. She was looking forward to getting to know him more.

"So how about we continue where we stopped?" Peter asked with a smirk. Maggie picked up a cowboy hat that was hanging on the wall behind her and threw it at his head, but he managed to duck in time. "Hey, what was that for?"

His phone rang. "Hold that thought." He picked up the phone and looked at the screen. "It's my son. I have a son, Ian, and a daughter, Cassie. Both married."

Now here was another reason Maggie wanted everything to slow down—there were children and families to get to know and consider, and yet all this talk of marriage was already floating around. Maggie couldn't help but feel trepidation. What if Peter's mother had told his son already?

"Should I take the call?" Peter asked.

"Do you think—"

He nodded. "There's a chance he might have heard if he's calling so soon. I was supposed to check in with him later in the evening. Should I answer? It's really up to you."

Maggie rubbed her eyes. *Aargh.* It seemed she wouldn't be able to get off this fast train even if she wanted to. She'd barely started this relationship with Peter, and dealing with his family so soon was a step she wasn't ready for, if the past was any indication. But it was possible his son hadn't heard about it. Yes, that was probably the case. "Okay."

Peter swiped the answer button and put the call on speakerphone. "Hello, Son."

"Dad, are you getting married?"

Maggie's heart dropped. Her nightmare had just come true.

CHAPTER 10

*P*eter looked at Maggie as if seeking permission, and she gave him a slight nod. "Yes, I am," he responded.

"Dad, are you crazy? Why am I just hearing about it, and from Grandmother instead of you?"

Peter stifled a sigh. It was just like he'd expected Ian to respond. "I'm fine, Son. I should have told you directly."

"Who is she?"

"Someone I've known for a very long time."

"Hello, Dad," a female voice chipped in.

Peter jerked back in surprise. His daughter was the last person he'd expected on the call. "Cassie?"

"Guilty as charged," she said in a cheeky tone.

"What are you doing at Ian's place?"

"Oh, he mentioned a certain somebody was getting married, and I figured it was better to have the conversation together. Congratulations!"

Now this was a surprise. "Thank you. Wait! Why are you so chirpy?"

"I love you, and I loved Mom, but it's about time."

"I don't agree with Cassie," Ian interjected.

"Why would you, since you're always getting daily *something-something* from your wife?" she threw back.

"Cassie!" Ian exclaimed. Peter just shook his head in wonder. "Who said that?"

Cassie chuckled. "Well, that's what you get for marrying my best friend. I think it would do Dad some good to get *some* before he gets too old to be in the game."

"Cassie, you're talking about your father here," Peter said in a disbelieving tone. "I'm not sure this is appropriate conversation, and I'm not that old."

"*Please.* We are married and ex-married people here. There's no shame in owning it."

Ian coughed to mask his discomfort at Cassie's words. Peter sensed Ian was going to try and steer the conversation back on track to bring up the main reason he'd called. Because there was one. "Well, Dad," he started, "I'll allow it, but only on one condition."

"And what might that be?"

"She has to sign a prenup."

CHAPTER 11

The line fell so silent Maggie could have heard a pin drop. It was the last thing she'd expected to hear, but she understood why. There were too many horror stories of gold diggers who'd robbed heirs of their inheritances.

"Really, Ian?" Cassie said. "I would think it's the other way around."

"What do you mean?"

"I did some digging based on Grandma's information. Did you know Margaret's son is a billionaire? We are super rich, but *not* that rich."

Maggie noticed Peter didn't even flinch. Like always, money had never really mattered that much to him. "She's not signing any prenup, and that's the end of it," he stated sternly. "I think this is the point where I introduce you guys to the love of my life. Ian, Cassie, say hello to Maggie Fields. Maggie, meet my wonderful children, Ian and Cassie."

"Oh, crap!" Ian said. "Why didn't you say so earlier? Now she'll think I'm a horrible person. Not cool, Dad."

Maggie held back a smile. "Nice to meet you too, Ian, and I don't think you're a horrible person, even though this conversation has been interesting. And I'm happy to sign a prenup if and when it comes to that."

"I don't agree," Peter insisted.

Maggie took Peter's hand and massaged it. She felt the tension in his body ease away with her touch. "I have more than enough money to last me a life-time, Peter, and I think it would give Ian the peace of mind he needs to know I'm not going to take away what rightfully belongs to him."

"Why don't you both sign a prenup?" Cassie suggested. "That would make it fair."

"I'm fine with that," Ian said.

"Well, I hate to disappoint you guys, but I plan to handle this issue myself," Peter responded. "But your opinion has been noted. Now, if you'll excuse me, I'd like to spend some time with my girlfriend."

"It was nice meeting you, Maggie," Cassie said. "We should get together for lunch sometime."

Maggie felt herself warm to her. "It would be my pleasure. Feel free to suggest a time and place that works for you."

"I will," Cassie responded. "And don't worry, Dad. I'll bring Grandma around. Just keep working your magic over there."

Peter laughed. "Bye, kids." He ended the call. "That went well."

Maggie leaned back. It could have been worse. "I'm glad it did, but this should have been a private conversation between your kids and yourself," Maggie said softly.

Peter ran a hand through his hair. Maggie's heart skipped a beat—he probably had no idea how dashing he looked. "I thought I'd have a chance to introduce you at the beginning of the call, but I had no idea the conversation would go the way it did."

Maggie chuckled. "Me too."

Peter smiled. "Cassie is something, isn't she?"

"I like her refreshing honesty."

Peter laughed. "If that's what you'd call it."

"She's wonderful."

"Yes, she is. What did you think about Ian?"

"I think his concerns are valid," Maggie said. "I

truly have more than enough money of my own. Max is good with investments, so I've earned a healthy return over the years."

"I don't know. It just rankled me. It's money I've worked hard for, and I'm entitled to spend it any way I like."

"I'm sure he's more concerned about the family wealth."

"The kids and grandkids can have it. I don't need it."

"Then you need to put that in writing. It's not a big deal. Really."

"I'll think about it."

Maggie knew when to stop pushing. "So how many grandkids do you have?"

"Two. Ian's daughter, Bella."

"Like the horse's name. She must be smart."

"Yes, she is. And then there's Caesar, Cassie's son," Peter said.

Maggie glanced at him in disbelief. "Caesar? As in Julius Caesar?"

"Yes, Cassie loves her Greek and Roman history."

She fought to hold back her chuckle. "I'm so sorry."

"Me too. But it could have been Aristotle."

Maggie dissolved into laughter. "You're kidding!"

"I kid you not. Cassie said, and I quote, 'It's perfect for character building.'"

"Oh my goodness."

"That's Cassie for you."

"She must have been a riot growing up."

"Yes, she was. I think I survived my wife's death because of her."

They both lapsed into silence. "What was her name?" Maggie asked after a while.

Peter twirled the ring on his finger before answering. "Emily."

It was a beautiful name. She had to be wonderful for Peter to have married her. "You must have loved her."

"Yes, I did. She found me when I thought I'd never see the light at the end of the tunnel. Eventually, little by little, she made me look forward to the next day."

The ache of the years she'd lost with Peter threatened to overcome her. "Your mother must have loved her."

Peter nodded. "She was so happy I'd recovered from a two-year depression that she didn't care who helped me."

So his mother had only been prejudiced against Maggie. The thought didn't sit well with her. Peter must have noticed because he took her hands in his. "I promise you, she won't stand in our way again. Do you believe me?"

She stared into his eyes, which bared the heart she'd missed so much. "I do."

Her phone rang right then.

Maggie sighed and checked the screen. It was an unknown number. Who could it possibly be? There was only one way to find out.

Maggie swiped the answer button.

CHAPTER 12

"Hello," Maggie said.

"Maggie, you have a boyfriend?" a familiar voice yelled through the speakerphone.

Maggie hung her head. Just when she'd thought she'd catch a break. "Becca? Why aren't you calling from your number?"

"This is the jet's satellite phone. It was either call you right now or turn the jet around like Max wanted."

Maggie chuckled and shook her head. These kids were nuts. "Hello, Max. I'm pretty sure you can hear me."

"Hey, Maggie. So, you have a boyfriend?"

"Yes, I do. His name is Peter Taylor, and he's right here."

"Hello, Peter," Becca said cheerily. "Nice to meet you."

"Nice to meet you guys too," Peter said.

"Peter Taylor? I've heard that name before. Are you a surgeon?" Max asked.

"Guilty as charged. How did you know?"

"I'm Max Dexin, Professor of Emergency Medicine at Dexington Medical. I think I met you once at a party the Dexingtons threw. I've heard about your great work in New York, sir."

"Oh, I remember you! You're the one opening up the ER Center."

"Yes, indeed."

"Interesting." Peter had that *look* on his face, the one that meant he was cooking up a new idea, though Maggie couldn't guess what it was. "I think we should have a chat when you get back."

"I would love to, sir."

"Great. Maggie will give you my number."

"I don't have your number," Maggie whispered.

"I'll give it to you," Peter whispered back.

Max and Becca laughed, while Maggie covered her face in embarrassment. The kids must have heard them. She had to change the subject. "So Dex told you guys?" she asked.

"We called him and heard him mumbling something about Maggie and a boyfriend under his breath," Max said. "So we forced him to spill the beans."

"I'm so happy for you!" Becca said. "So when is the wedding? I need to get it on my schedule." Becca was an event planner and had pulled off many celebrity weddings.

"Becca!" Maggie and Max said together.

"Max, you need to chill. Maggie has a love life now, just like you and I. Or do you not expect her to get married at some point like we did?" Becca scolded.

"Definitely not like us," Max mumbled. "We were married and didn't even know it. Maggie, you can't get hitched in Vegas like us. Promise me you'll wait till we get back."

Maggie shook her head in disbelief. She hadn't expected the kids to go off the rails just because she had a man in her life.

"Maggie, promise me, okay?"

My goodness, he was really serious. "I will," Maggie promised.

"Good. Dr. Taylor, it was nice meeting you."

"It's Peter. Same here."

"Nice meeting you too," Becca echoed. "Maggie, we need to get off the phone now. I can see Chloe is waking up, and this call will never end if she gets on it."

Maggie laughed because it was so true. "I'll talk to you later. Safe travels."

"Bye," they echoed. The line went dead.

"That wasn't so bad," Maggie said.

"They sound like nice kids."

"They truly are."

"So you want to get hitched in Vegas?"

"Oh, please. Don't start."

Peter grinned. "I had to try." Then his face turned serious as he held her gaze. He probably could guess at what bothered her. "Everything is going to turn out fine," he said. "We'll take it slow and get to know each other and our families."

"And the Dexingtons."

Peter gave Maggie a quizzical look. "The Dexingtons? Why?"

"The boys found out a few months ago that they're related to them."

"Now that's something my mother would be happy about."

"I bet."

"Don't be cynical." Peter tickled her. "We'll take whatever small wins we can get."

Maggie laughed and playfully pushed his hands

away. "Stop it. Please. Wait, I think I hear something."

"You just want me to stop." Peter wrapped his arms around her. "I love you, Mae, and we'll get through this."

Maggie saw the love shining through his eyes. "I love you too, Peter. Thank you for coming back into my life." Then her eyes darted toward the barn door. The rumble of a motorcycle grew louder and echoed in the air. "I think the mechanic is here."

"Would it be okay if I stayed the rest of the weekend after he finishes fixing my car?" Peter asked.

Maggie gave him a bright smile. "That would be perfect."

Then she proceeded to give him a French kiss that promised love, hope, and a future of figuring things out together.

EPILOGUE

"*H*appy married life!" everyone shouted as they waved Maggie and Peter farewell from where they stood near the helipad on the ranch. The newly minted Taylors were about to hop into the helicopter that would fly them to the private jet that would then take them to their first honeymoon destination—a private beach on one of the islands of Turks and Caicos.

The whole family was there to see them off—the Taylors, the Dexins, the Dexingtons, Peter's friends and colleagues, and folks from town and church. Only the dragon lady was missing—she'd begged off with a headache after the church service.

Maggie felt her face and neck grow warm all the way to the roots of her hair. But she didn't care, because she was married to the hunk beside her, who looked so delectable in a T-shirt and jeans with matching cowboy hat and boots. Who said silver foxes were not the finest? They only got better with age.

Peter held Maggie's hand as they made their way to where the helicopter waited. "We did it," he whispered and snuck a kiss on her cheek.

Maggie chuckled. Yes, they'd done it. Their thirty-two-year dream had finally become a reality. Maggie and Peter had dated for three months and could have gone much longer, except Maggie had caught the marriage bug and indicated she was ready.

By then, all the kids had come around. Even Ian had made his peace with Peter and dropped the prenup idea. But Maggie had insisted on it and that was that. Once dragon lady found out the Dexins were related to the Dexingtons, she'd given her approval just like Peter had predicted.

Peter had chosen to retire from the New York hospital where he'd worked, to focus fully on his research, but a conversation later and Max had convinced him to join the board of the ER Center as its first chairman. He'd agreed. He'd also taken to the ranch like a duck to water and spent so many mornings riding horses with both Chloe and Maggie that

Chloe had announced she'd adopted him as her new grandfather.

Max had built Maggie and Peter a house on the property near her favorite spot as their wedding present, with enough space to host their kids whenever they visited. Becca had promised the house would be ready by the time they returned from their three-month honeymoon. They'd chosen to keep Peter's house in New York for whenever they visited the other half of their grandkids.

Maggie had thought her life was full, but the Lord had worked a miracle and enriched her life beyond her imagination.

Now she had a man that loved her with all his heart.

Her very own Cowboy Doctor.

Dex leaned against the beam and stared out of his floor-to-ceiling windows at the land below—the land that he'd nurtured and cared for over the years with his brothers. It had been a long, winding road to raise the ranch to its current status, but it had been worth it.

But that wasn't what occupied his thoughts as he

held a glass of water in his hands and looked out far into the mountains. All he could think about was the happiness he'd seen on Maggie's face earlier today as she leaned against Peter, the joy and laughter from Max and Becca at Chloe's antics, and the longing in his own heart for a wife and a family of his own.

He'd met women both at college and in his travels all over the country on behalf of the ranch, and he'd gone out on a date or two with some of them. Still, he hadn't found a woman who made his heart skip a beat, a lady that loved him for who he was and not for what he had.

Sure, he wasn't as outgoing as Jax, or as handsome as Max, and he was more introspective than any other members of his family, yet there had to be a woman out there—someone who appreciated his hands that worked the land, the person whom he could give his whole heart to, and who would be willing to spend the rest of her life with him on the ranch.

Because unlike his brothers, Dex knew the land and he were one. He could feel its heartbeat, knew this was his calling, and couldn't imagine living anywhere else.

But time was running out on him. He wasn't a

spring chicken by any means, yet he'd never felt the longing for a family of his own until now.

Change was in the air, with the construction of the Dexin ER Center coming to an end and the hospital opening soon. Dexin Valley would grow and adapt to accommodate the flood of new employees from all over the country.

Maybe she was one of those that would come.

Maybe now was the Lord's timing.

And maybe, just maybe, he would meet her soon.

Thank you so much for reading! Want to know how Dex found love (in a blind date romance)?

Check out A DOCTOR BLIND DATE FOR THE COWBOY at https://thebookishdobi.com.

An excerpt:

Zoey Brown froze, her face warming up more than the hot Saturday sun she'd just walked in from. How could this have happened to her today, of all days?

"Ma'am, your skirt's ripped," the cool baritone voice repeated quietly from behind her.

Zoey bristled even as the scented smell of cleaning supplies from the nearby detergent aisle assaulted her nostrils. Yes, she'd heard him the first time. Did he have to say it again? She fought the urge to reach back and touch the rip that had appeared as she'd leaned forward to place her groceries on the checkout counter.

It served her right. She should have just stuck with the pants and jeans that had been her uniform for over a decade. Instead, she'd opted for a black skirt and a sleeveless peach blouse, which went wonderfully with her sun-kissed skin, for a change. Today's weather forecast had predicted it would be the hottest day of summer. Who knew the universe would reward her efforts with this unwanted publicity on her first day in Dexin Valley?

Zoey bit her lip. She couldn't continue standing here, pretending nothing was wrong. How was she going to get herself out of this pickle?

Her jacket was in her car, too far away to reach without taking a walk of shame through the store and out into the parking lot. How could she deal with this in the gracious manner her step-mother liked to harp on without becoming the day's side show in the tiny grocery store that seemed to serve half of the town's population right now?

She could feel the curious gazes from the other shoppers around her. It didn't help that this was the day she'd worn her comfy white granny underwear instead of the more sophisticated lingerie that filled her wardrobe. Now all it did was serve as a white flag against the contrasting black skirt, calling attention to the tear.

Something fell on Zoey's shoulders, and she flinched. She looked down only to see a dark brown plaid shirt—long enough to extend beyond the hem of her skirt—resting on her shoulders. It carried the faint scent of sweet hay, leather, and fresh grass, a fragrance that seemed to warm her more than the shirt itself.

Zoey turned in relief to see who the owner was, and her eyes met the warmest brown eyes she'd ever seen—twin mirrors that seemed to reach down into her soul. The broad-chested young man towered over her five-foot-seven frame, and his eyes held a look of concern as they searched her face.

"Hope you don't mind, ma'am," he said in the same voice she'd heard earlier, gesturing to the shirt. "Are you okay?" he asked in the same voice she'd heard earlier...

Want to read more? You can grab A DOCTOR BLIND DATE FOR THE COWBOY at https://dobidaniels.com!

Check out all Dobi Daniels books at https://dobidaniels.com.

ACKNOWLEDGMENTS

Writing a book is harder and more rewarding than I could have ever imagined. And it would not have been possible without the support, love, and encouragement from my number one cheerleader, my dearest mom. My life would never have been this awesome and wonderful without you.

Of course, I have to thank my precious little DC for his smiles and antics. You brighten my day and give me the strength to keep pushing through.

Thank you to my sisters for encouraging me on this wonderful journey. And a special thanks to my baby brother (who is so not a baby anymore) for being super supportive and checking in on my progress. You guys are the best.

Thank you to my wonderful author friends. You know who you are. Your selflessness and willingness to share what you know has made my writing journey smoother and an exciting one. And a special thanks to my ARC readers whose support have made a difference.

Most of all, I want to thank God who gave me life, surrounded me with the most wonderful people, and loved me all the way. You make my life complete.

And finally, a special thanks to all my readers whose love of my stories spur me on to write more. Thank you!

ABOUT DOBI DANIELS

As a former physician and business executive in another life—with a childhood filled with reading multi-genre novels—Dobi Daniels loves to write sweet thrilling romance stories with heart. She enjoys dreaming up everyday characters who rise above unfavorable circumstances to overcome incredible odds and find joy along the way.

When not writing, Dobi can be found binging K-dramas and ice cream with her little sidekick by her side.

A Doctor Second Chance for the Rancher is the prequel to A Cowboy Loves the Doctor Series, Dobi's second romance series.

Thanks for reading A DOCTOR SECOND CHANCE FOR THE RANCHER!
https://dobidaniels.com

hello@dobidaniels.com
facebook.com/dobidaniels
instagram.com/dobidaniels

www.ingramcontent.com/pod-product-compliance
Lightning Source LLC
Chambersburg PA
CBHW010612310726
48969CB00010B/2671